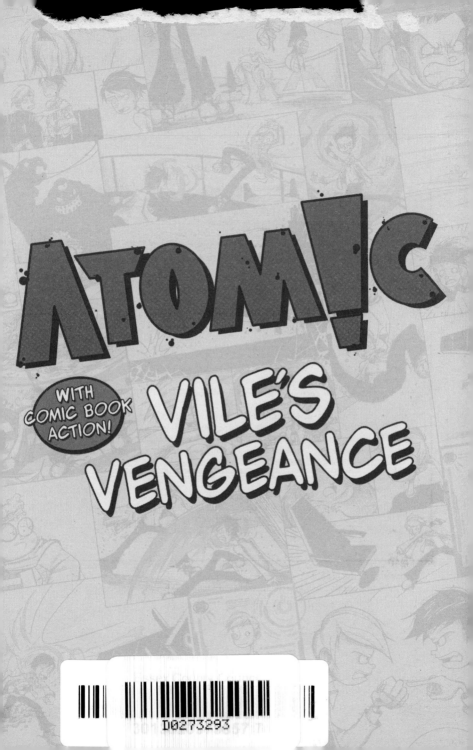

To Ruth, for being SUPER.

Scholastic Children's Books
An imprint of Scholastic Ltd
Euston House, 24 Eversholt Street
London, NW1 1DB, UK
Registered office: Westfield Road, Southam, Warwickshire, CV47 0RA
SCHOLASTIC and associated logos are trademarks and/or registered
trademarks of Scholastic Inc.

First published in the UK by Scholastic Ltd, 2012
This edition published by Scholastic Ltd, 2015

Text copyright © Guy Bass, 2012
Illustrations copyright © Jamie Littler, 2012

The rights of Guy Bass and Jamie Littler to be identified as the
author and illustrator of this work have been asserted by them.

Cover illustration © Jamie Littler, 2012

ISBN 978 1407 14804 5

Printed and bound by CPI Group (UK) Ltd, Croydon CR0 4YY
Papers used by Scholastic Children's Books are made from wood grown
in sustainable forests.

1 3 5 7 9 10 8 6 4 2

www.scholastic.co.uk
www.guybass.com

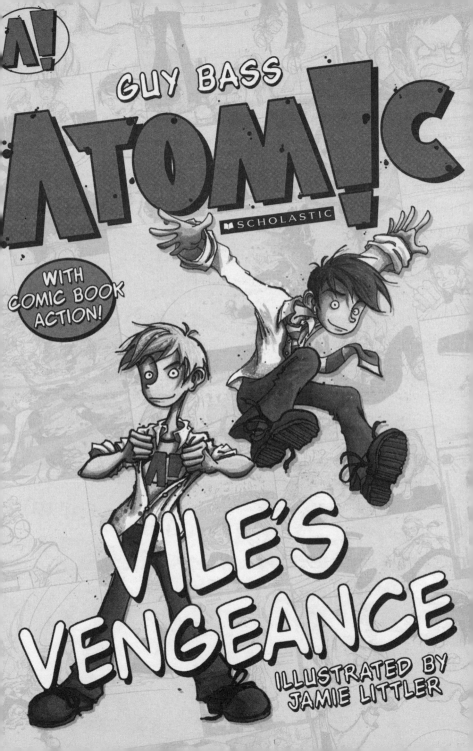

OMIC
URES
MMON COLD

"It came to me on the toilet," reveals superhero scientist

Atomic Refuses to Sell "Multi-Gun" Technology to Military
Fifty-seven-setting weapon "not for sale", claims Atomic

IC BOMBER"

Atomic Celebrates Ten Years of Brilliance

(by Saving World From Giant Monster)

"It's all in a decade's work," says world's most impressive man

Atomic "Too Busy For Family"

Captain Atomic said yesterday he was too busy saving the world to think about having a relationship, never mind having kids. "Oh, sure, I'd love to meet Ms Right and start a family, but as long as the world needs me, I don't have the time..."

!
e's
ats
y?

DAY ONE:

GARGANTUS, THE TWELVE-TENTACLED TITAN
MADE FROM TERROR

Albion City Telegraph

3RD SEPTEMBER (EARLY EDITION)

EVERYTHING FINE

There's Nothing to Worry About, Says Everyone

THE NEAR FUTURE

It was the same day that the 777th Interferion Intergalactic Invasion Fleet invaded Earth. Fortunately, their entire space fleet was smaller than a grain of sand, so no one noticed.

It was also the day that Earth's 856th superhero put on his costume for the very first time. He called himself The Flaming Piglet. (He was neither.)

And it was the day that supervillain and all-round bad egg Vinister Vile attacked Albion City for the nineteenth time.

The attack began at 8.01 a.m. with these words:

"Citizens of Albion City, your day of destruction is upon you! Behold, GARGANTUS, the twelve-tentacled titan made from terror!"

After that, it was what you'd expect from one of Vinister Vile's attacks – a giant monster appeared out of the ground, and then there was lots of running and screaming from terrified onlookers.

"Dumbfounded dimwits! Always depending on a daring do-gooder to defeat my dastardly designs! But nothing can delay your downfall!" cried Vile, hovering over the hundred-metre monstrosity in his bio-copter, The Creepy Crawler.

Gargantus had trampled its eighth car and swatted its third police helicopter before Captain

Atomic arrived, soaring through the air wearing his patented rocket pack. It was then that Vile heard the words he always longed to hear. Which, as it happens, were also the words he feared the most:

"Not so fast, Vinister Vile!"

FAR FROM ORDINARY

EARTHQUAKE REPORTED IN DOWNTOWN ALBION CITYCRACKS APPEAR IN MAIN STREET**CITIZENS TOLD NOT TO PANIC, EVERYTHING PROBABLY STILL FINE**

Twelve minutes earlier on that very same day, on a vast, invisible island floating above Albion City, two boys were trying on their school uniforms.

"We look *stupid*," said Tommy, staring at himself in the mirror.

ATOMIC FILES

NAME: Tommy Atomic

AGE: 10

EYES: Green

HAIR: Black

POWERS AND ABILITIES:

Level 6 Telekenisis –

subject can lift, move

and repel objects with

the power of his mind.

Can also create force

fields and fly at speeds of up to 129 kph.

[Note: Subject's Mental Powers are inherited from his

mother's side (refer to file: Madame Malice).]

Subject also possesses genius-level intellect. Excels in

quantum dynamics, materials chemistry and sudoku.

Tommy was dressed in a neat blue blazer and red-and-yellow striped tie. He ruffled his jet-black hair and squirmed as if he was trying to escape from his clothes.

"This is **SO NOT WHAT I MEANT** when I said I wanted to spend more time **AWAY FROM THE ISLAND**. I mean, **SCHOOL? REALLY?**"

"I like it," said Jonny, nudging his twin brother out of the way.
Jonny flattened his bright blond hair to his head and straightened his tie. He couldn't help but smile. He'd never looked so . . .

NORMAL!

ATOMIC FILES

NAME: Jonny Atomic

AGE: 10

EYES: Green

HAIR: Blond

POWERS AND ABILITIES:

Super-strength,

super-speed and high

resistance to physical

injury. Can lift a double-decker

bus or smash a hole in a brick wall (can also then eat the

brick without getting tummy trouble).

[Note: Power levels as yet undetermined – subject shows

reluctance to explore full extent of abilities.]

"You *would* like it. It's your stupid fault we're in this mess," grumbled Tommy. "We should be training to be **SUPERHEROES** right now. But *no* – thanks to your constant begging, Dad's sending us to school. *Nice* one."

"At least we'll be off the Island. Anything's better than being stuck here till we're grown-ups," replied Jonny, stepping out of the room on to a large round balcony. "Anyway, maybe Dad wants us to see what it's like to be **ORDINARY**. **I DON'T KNOW IF YOU'VE NOTICED, BUT WE DON'T GET A LOT OF ORDINARY AROUND HERE.**"

"Oh me, oh my! Don't you look smart!" said a voice. They looked down to see a small brown and white hamster sitting on the floor.

"Morning, Aunt Sandwich," said Jonny and Tommy together.

ATOMIC FILES

NAME: Aunt Sandwich

AGE: 44 (Hamster years)

EYES: Brown

HAIR: Brown and white

POWERS AND ABILITIES:

Subject has scientifically-increased intelligence and the ability to speak.

Qualified Atomic Bomber pilot.

Can store up to four chestnuts in each cheek.

"Hang on, I'll get the camera. Your dad will want to see you all dressed up!" giggled the hamster. She clapped her paws together and scurried down a nearby staircase to the floor below.

"See? This is *exactly* what I'm talking about," said Jonny.

The boys peered over the balcony. Below them was a huge oval room. In the centre stood a large meeting table and several chairs. On one wall of the room was a huge crescent-shaped window looking out to sky and white clouds. Far below them, the vast skyscrapers of Albion City gleamed in the morning sun.

"We live on a giant, invisible floating island. Mum's in prison for trying to take over the world. Our uncle and aunt are talking animals. Then there's Dad. . ." continued Jonny. "Let's face it – we're about as far from ordinary as you can get."

ATOMIC FILES

NAME: Uncle Dogday

AGE: 63 (Dog years)

EYES: Brown

HAIR: Black and grey

POWERS AND ABILITIES:

Scientifically-increased intelligence and the ability to speak.

Chess grandmaster.

Fully house-trained.

"It wasn't my fault! Tommy—" began Jonny.

"I don't care whose fault it was, or who started it," retorted Uncle Dogday. "You're too powerful to be barrelling around here like a couple of bears. I thought we agreed that you would confine your scuffles to the Training Arena after the . . . *incident* in the Core Chamber."

"Sorry, Uncle Dogday," said Jonny and Tommy in humble unison.

"Stop fussing, Dogday. Boys will be boys!" chuckled Aunt Sandwich, reappearing with a tiny camera. She sat back on her hind legs and held the camera up. "Say 'cheese'!"

CLICK!

"Do you think Dad will be back in time to take us to school?" asked Tommy.

"Let's have a look, shall we? Screen!" barked

Uncle Dogday, and a large image appeared in the centre of the window, showing news footage of a tiny, flying figure doing battle with a twelve-tentacled monster.

"We're coming to you live from Albion City, where Captain Atomic is facing yet another of Vinister Vile's mad monsters!" said the news reporter. "Atomic never backs down from an encounter with his arch-enemy, and Vile never seems to learn his lesson. It looks like it's going to be one heck of a fight!"

"Sorry, boys," said Uncle Dogday. "It doesn't look like your father will be giving you a lift to school today."

BEING ATOMIC

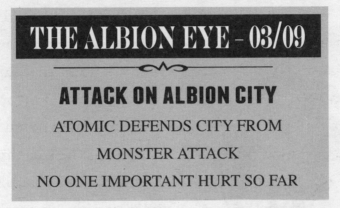

THE ALBION EYE – 03/09

ATTACK ON ALBION CITY

ATOMIC DEFENDS CITY FROM

MONSTER ATTACK

NO ONE IMPORTANT HURT SO FAR

Tommy sighed as he and his brother climbed into one of their father's Atomic Bombers. He had hoped that, for once, his dad might have stopped saving the world long enough to take them to their first day at school.

It was always the same – something always

seemed to get in the way . . . but as their granddad used to say, "It's not easy being a member of this family." It was certainly a mixed blessing – the Atomics had never gone in for masks and costumes and code names. They left that to superheroes Miss Mystery and The Unknown Quantity. As a result, Captain Atomic was a household name by the time he was three years old. His own father had introduced him to heroics at an early age. It was all he had ever known.

But when Captain Atomic had sons of his own, he decided to keep their existence a secret. In fact, no one outside the family knew that Jonny and Tommy Atomic had even been born.

"You'll have plenty of time for heroics – and *super*heroics – when you're older," Captain Atomic always told his boys. "I have powerful enemies. If they knew about you, they would do everything they could to find you. I can't risk my enemies discovering my . . . weakness."

Tommy didn't like the idea of being a "weakness". He longed to show his dad – and the rest of the world – exactly how powerful he was.

"Now promise me, no powers at school," said Uncle Dogday, as the boys strapped themselves into their seats.

"We promise," said Jonny and Tommy together, although Tommy made sure to cross his fingers behind his back.

"And remember – down there, you're not Jonny and Tommy Atomic – you're Jonny and Tommy Smith."

"*Smith?* That's the most boring secret identity ever! Can't we be called something cool like Laserblaze or Dragondeath?"

"I'm not sure your father would approve of Dragondeath . . . in any case, you're not supposed to be different. You are two *very* ordinary ten-year-olds who have just moved to the area," continued Uncle Dogday.

"Oh me, oh my, it's all *so* exciting!" said Aunt Sandwich, scurrying into the pilot's seat.

"Oh, and one more thing," added Uncle Dogday, as the Atomic Bomber hummed with magnetic energy. "*Try* not to destroy the school."

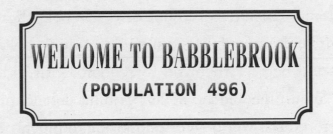

WELCOME TO BABBLEBROOK

(POPULATION 496)

THE BABBLEBROOK BABBLE
3rd September

BABBLEBROOK NAMED

"WORLD'S SLEEPIEST VILLAGE"

"It's dead boring – and that's just the way we like it,"

say locals

The Atomic Bomber soared at much-faster-than-the-speed-of-sound across the morning sky, its in-built imperceptors rendering it invisible to the naked eye.

Jonny Atomic stared out of the bubble-shaped craft and grinned. He still couldn't quite believe his dad had let them go to school! Until today, the only time they ever left Atomic Island (and explored the world their dad spent so much time protecting) was on their weekly day trips to the zoo, park or museum with Uncle Dogday and Aunt Sandwich. For Jonny, those outings gave him the chance to pretend he was ordinary, and allowed him to imagine what it would be like to live among normal people. Tommy was a different matter – spending time with ordinary people just convinced him how much *better* he was than everyone else.

"Why do we have to be so far away from Albion City?" asked Tommy as they sped over green fields. "Nothing *happens* in the countryside."

"That's the idea," said Aunt Sandwich. "Cities are full of supervillains – there's no point in delivering you right into their hands, is there?

Oh me, oh my!"

"We can take care of ourselves – Dad knows that," moaned Tommy. "He'd saved the world *twice* by the time he was our age. Why doesn't he trust us? There are a million more heroic things we could be doing. Unless. . ."

"Unless what?" Jonny asked.

"Unless this is some kind of *test*. Like a – a challenge, to see if we've got what it takes to be heroes."

"Here we go." Jonny shook his head. "You always have to make life more complicated than it is. Not everything's about powers and heroics and saving the day, Tommy."

"Think about it – why did Dad suddenly change his mind? Because of your nagging? No *way*. Why waste our time in some stupid school for 'normals'? He might as well leave us on the Island. Unless there's some reason, something we're meant to do. Something . . . *super*."

"Would you listen to yourself?" said Jonny. "That is exactly the opposite of why we're here! We're here to go to school! We're here to—"

"We're here!" cried Aunt Sandwich, as the Bomber touched down in the middle of a small village green.

"Where *is* 'here'?" asked Tommy, peering out of the Bomber window.

"Welcome to Babblebrook – isn't it just charming?" chirped Aunt Sandwich. "And do you see that large building on the other side of the village green? *That* is your new school."

Jonny and Tommy could see a large, old-looking building with a square car park in front of it. A few children were making their way inside, dressed in identical blue blazers.

"Chestnuts! I almost forgot!" said Aunt Sandwich, opening a compartment with her paw and scurrying in. She scampered back out, carrying two watches in her teeth, and dropped them on the boys' laps. "Atomic Clocks! Your dad wanted you to have these, just in case. They're long-range-signal watches – only to be used in *dire emergencies*. Press the red button to send a signal back to Atomic Island, as well as to the other watch. Oh, and they've also got a calculator, satnav and Tetris! Oh me, oh my!"

"Thanks," said Jonny, as they fixed the watches to their wrists. He shot Tommy a stern look. "I'm sure we won't need them."

"Well then, what are you waiting for? I'll pick you up at three-thirty!" said Aunt Sandwich, opening the Bomber hatch as they heard the distant clanging of the school bell.

"Race you!" said Tommy suddenly, and propelled himself towards the school as fast as a cheetah.

"Tommy, no pow—" began Jonny, but Tommy was long gone. Jonny shook his head, and tried his best to run at "normal" speed towards the school.

MS CRACKDOWN

Albion Today

YOUR CITY'S LOCAL E-PAPER

3rd September

ATOMIC LEAVES GARGANTUS COLD
Uses multi-gun's freeze ray to
put monster on ice

"LOOK OUT!"

cried Tommy, skidding to a halt outside the school gates and almost knocking over a small, round boy who was trying to pluck up the courage to go inside. He had short, curly ginger hair and wore thick glasses that made his eyes look enormous. He was wearing a bright yellow cape tied around his neck and had a small plastic water pistol clipped on to his belt.

"NICE RAY GUN!"

said Tommy. "Are you a superhero?"

"Who, me? Uh – I—" began the boy, nervously.

"'Cause you're not going to find many supervillains in . . . Bubblebrick, or wherever we are," continued Tommy. "And you should lose the cape. My dad says capes are kind of . . . villainous."

"Your dad?" said the boy.

"He says all that cape-swishing is just a way of disguising their insecurities. You should get a rocket pack instead. My dad—"

"IGNORE HIM!"

interrupted Jonny, finally catching up to his brother. He couldn't believe Tommy was already risking their identity – they weren't even inside the school yet!

"I'm Jonny – Jonny *Smith*. That's my name. He's Tommy. Our dad couldn't bring us, but just for a really normal reason, like he started early this morning in his totally normal job doing totally normal stuff."

"Wow, you're *really* good at this," said Tommy, sarcastically.

"IT'S MY FIRST DAY TOO,"

said the boy, staring nervously at the school entrance. "I'm Vernon – Vernon Vincent."

ATOMIC FILES

NAME: Vernon Vincent

AGE: 9¾

EYES: Grey-blue

HAIR: Red

DESCRIPTION: Pupil at Jonny and Tommy's school.

Newly enrolled.

THREAT LEVEL: 0

POWERS AND ABILITIES: None known.

"Don't worry – how bad can it be?" said Jonny with a smile. "Come on, let's see what all the fuss is about. . ."

The boys hurried inside, but no sooner were they through the door, when. . .

"NO RUNNING!"

The three boys screeched to a halt. At the end of a long corridor stood a tall, neatly dressed woman with a large flame of impossibly shiny, red hair and pointy, dark-rimmed glasses. She fixed her burning glare upon them.

"Scuttling like beetles. . ." Her voice hissed like a snake. "Running is the enemy of obedience, and *Ms Crackdown* will be obeyed."

ATOMIC FILES

NAME: Anita Crackdown (Ms)

AGE: 59

EYES: Green

HAIR: Red

DESCRIPTION: Teacher at Jonny and Tommy's School.

THREAT LEVEL: 1 (Possible detention danger)

POWERS AND ABILITIES: None known.

"Sorry, uh, miss," began Jonny. "We didn't want to be—"

"NO TALKING either!" barked Ms Crackdown. "Running . . . talking . . . you clearly haven't been *broken in* yet. Which class are you in? Mr Gentle's? Miss Goodacre's? Those *fools*. They haven't got the first clue how to deal with children."

"We're new," said Tommy, boldly. "As in, *really* new. We have no idea what you're talking about."

Ms Crackdown stared at Tommy, who stared back and smiled broadly.

"Ah, you're the fresh meat for the mincer – *excellent*," she growled. "You're with me. This way, beetles."

The bewildered boys followed Ms Crackdown down a long corridor and up two flights of stairs, as her piercing voice rang out.

"If you wish to survive here, you would do well to take heed of The Crackdown Rules," continued

Ms Crackdown. "ONE! You are not children – you are *insects* . . . grubs . . . larvae, nothing more and I am the boot that steps on you. The sooner you understand that, the better. TWO! There is nothing I hate more in a child than *confidence*. It is a sign that I still have work to do. THREE! If you have a problem, take it to someone who cares. I promise you, that person is not me."

Jonny and Tommy looked at each other as they reached their new classroom. Were *all* teachers like this?

"Welcome to my world," hissed Ms Crackdown, opening the classroom door. The boys stepped inside and were met by the fearful eyes of twenty-one nine-year-olds. A deep sense of impending dread filled the room.

"Sit over there, by the window," huffed Ms Crackdown. She waved her hand as if it was hard work. "Class, this is Twin A, Twin B and Four-eyes."

"My name's—" began Tommy.

"Do not even *attempt* to tell me your real name, Twin B, it will only make you feel more important than you are. I make a point of only naming lifeless objects. Look out of the window. Do you see that blue car?"

The boys stared out. A rusty, electric-blue car

was parked right next to the school.

"That is Sir Percival," continued Ms Crackdown, her voice softening slightly. "I named my car because lifeless objects are reliable and trustworthy. Children, however, are ticking time bombs of expectation and high hopes, and must be reminded of their failings at all costs."

"I want to go home," whispered a terrified Vernon as he sat down.

"Thank you, Four-eyes. You just reminded me of rule FOUR!" Ms Crackdown barked. "If you wish to speak, raise your hand. I will then decide whether you deserve my attention, which you probably won't."

Tommy raised his hand. Ms Crackdown stared at him.

"Yes?" she snapped.

"Is it too late to join another class?" asked Tommy.

"Tommy. . .!" whispered Jonny.

Ms Crackdown took a deep, whistling breath through her nostrils.

"A willful creature, are you?" she said, finally. "Well, we'll soon change that."

She took out a stack of papers and began handing them around the class. "Now, because it is the first day of term – and to ensure that any lingering memories of your oh-so-happy, Mummy-and-Daddy-took-me-to-the-beach-and-bought-me-an-ice-cream summer holidays are wiped from your minds – I have prepared a test for you. Not for any good reason, but because I can. You have ten minutes. If you do not pass, I will personally call your parents and tell them how lazy, stupid and ugly you are."

There was a stifled groan as Ms Crackdown handed out the last test paper with a "Well, don't just gawp at it, woodlice – *begin*."

As Jonny stared at the questions, he started to wonder whether being ordinary was all it was cracked up to be. A test in the first hour of his first day of school? He'd never been good at tests. Even the predictable ones set by Uncle Dogday (which were almost *always* about dogs) were a challenge. Tommy had always been better at this sort of thing, and Jonny often felt no one expected him to be good at anything except smashing things to pieces. Still, he wasn't about to give up. If this was what ordinary people did, then he was going to do his best. He grabbed his pen and—

"Finished!" came a cry. Tommy was twiddling his pen in his one hand and waving the paper in the other.

"Finished? What do you mean, 'finished'?" snarled Ms Crackdown, grabbing his paper. She returned to her desk, took out a bright red pen and started marking.

"What are you doing? You were supposed to go slowly!" whispered Jonny.

"I *did* go slowly." Tommy sat back in his chair. "I took *twice* as long as I needed. What was I meant to do, pretend not to know the answers? It was *easy*."

"But we're supposed to be fitting in! You—" began Jonny, as Ms Crackdown threw down her pen and got to her feet.

"Twin B! How *dare* you cheat in my classroom," sneered Ms Crackdown.

"Cheat? *Please*. I didn't cheat," laughed Tommy.

"Don't try to deny it! The only way you could possibly have passed my test so quickly is by dishonest means. Come now, confess – how did you do it?"

"I didn't cheat!" repeated Tommy. "Your stupid

test just wasn't hard enough."

"Misguided worm," said Ms Crackdown. "They all think they can take me on at first. They all think they're special. But you don't stand a chance against me, I have been in this business too long," snarled Ms Crackdown.

"Maybe you should retire," said Tommy, narrowing his eyes. The whole class gasped and Vernon even began sliding under his desk in terror. Ms Crackdown took another whistling breath and ground her teeth.

"Sorry, Ms Crackdown, my brother is just a bit nervous!" blurted Jonny, shooting Tommy his sternest look. "You know, first day of school. . .!"

"Nervous? Well, *fear* is the one thing I like to encourage in my pupils," replied Ms Crackdown. "Every weekend I climb into Sir Percival and I drive fifty kilometres to the local zoo. For three hours I stand outside the reptile enclosure and dare myself to go inside . . . to conquer my chronic *fear of crocodiles*. One day, perhaps. . ."

"Wow, didn't see *that* coming," chuckled Tommy.

"She's bonkers," whimpered a terrified Vernon, as Ms Crackdown took another whistling breath. Finally, she said:

"The classroom is like an ants' nest – the actions of one affect the whole. Thus, the fate of one must be the fate of all. Therefore, you will *all* complete a three-hundred-word essay entitled *Why I Am an Ant*. And tomorrow, another essay. And the day after that, and after that, and so on, until Twin B admits he cheated and spares you all."

"What? That's not fair!" Tommy all but got up from his seat. "They haven't done anything! You can't punish them as well – it isn't right."

"Then the answer is simple, you little grub," she said. "Admit you cheated."

"I didn't cheat!" he snapped.

"Admit it," repeated Ms Crackdown. "Or everyone else will be punished for your selfish actions. *Surrender!*"

Tommy looked around at the faces of his classmates. Jonny clenched his fist until his knuckles cracked. After a moment, Tommy grinned and turned back to Ms Crackdown and stared into her eyes.

"*Never,*" he said.

VERNON'S COMIC

ALBION CITY SUN SAYS:

Vinister VILEST

Sun votes Vile World's Most Hated Villain

"Everyone in the world is stupid and rubbish
and smells of cheesy old socks! Shut up!"
villain might have said as he fled scene of crime

Albion City Bulletin 03/09

Vanquished Vinister Vile Vanishes

Atomic fails to capture arch-enemy

after defeating Gargantus in Albion City

It was fair to say that Jonny's first day at school
wasn't going quite as planned. He had imagined
making friends with everyone in his class, enjoying

lessons, playing games and finding out as much as he could about normal life. But thanks to Tommy – and a morning of silent essay writing – no one would talk to either of them.

"What are you so grumpy about?" asked Tommy, tucking into his lunch as they sat alone on a table in the corner of the school hall.

"Shut up. I'm not talking to you ever again," said Jonny. He added, "Dad said no powers. He's going to *kill* you."

"Oh, *come* on. So I'm good at tests – so what? It's not like I've told everyone who we are," said Tommy.

"We've only been here three hours and everyone hates us! Just tell Ms Crackdown you cheated. Tell her you're sorry."

"You are *such* a baby," replied Tommy. "Don't you get it? This is it – this is the test!"

"What test?"

"The test! The *real* test – the one I was telling you about – the whole reason Dad sent us to this stupid back-end-of-nowhere school in the first place! I worked it out just after Ms Crackdown called us 'worthless slugs'. *This* is why we're here! This is the first challenge on our way to being superheroes – *defeating the evil Ms Crackdown*."

Jonny gripped the side of the table so hard it cracked.

"OK, A) you're *insane*," Jonny growled. "And B), what are you *talking* about? Do you know how paranoid you sound? Ms Crackdown's not evil! She's a teacher!"

"Oh come on, she's barmy! Classic supervillain material. How many teachers do you know who call their pupils 'insects'?"

"I don't know any teachers!" spat Jonny. "Nor do you! You don't know anything about anything. Why can't you let things be what they are? You're going to *ruin* this."

"I'm doing what's right – what Dad wants us to do. I'm standing up against the villain. I just have to find a way to defeat her – a weakness."

"She's just a mean old lady!" cried Jonny, getting up from his chair. "You know that I've been looking forward to this for months and you're just doing this to spoil everything! It's always the. . . Oh, just forget it."

"Come on, Jonny, you know I'm right!" called Tommy, but Jonny had already wandered out into the field behind the hall.

Outside, Jonny did his best to calm down. He took a moment to appreciate the fact that at least he wasn't 1.2 kilometres above the earth on an invisible floating island. Then he spotted Vernon sitting on his own under a tree, his face buried in a comic book. Jonny wandered over and sat down next to him.

"How's your first day going?" he asked with a smile.

"OK, I suppose," replied Vernon. "Except for all the tests."

"Yeah, sorry about that – my brother likes to show off," grumbled Jonny. "Do you have any brothers or sisters?"

"No," replied Vernon, fiddling with his water pistol.

Jonny and Vernon sat in silence for a few moments, watching the other children running around, both wondering if and when they would be able to join in.

"So, you like comics?" asked Jonny, finally.

"*Superhero* comics," replied Vernon, perking up. "I only collect superhero comics – the *official* ones, the *actual* adventures of *real* superheroes. So, like, *The Masquerade*, *The Grim Ghoul*, *Tom Morrow – Man From the Future*, *The League of Cavemen*,

Mr V, Miss Mystery—"

"What's that one?" asked Jonny, pointing to the comic in Vernon's hand. Vernon held it up. On the cover was a picture of a man wearing a rocket pack shooting a giant robot with a ray gun.

"No *way* – Dad?" said Jonny.

"Dad?" repeated Vernon.

"I mean, dead! Dead . . . good comic! I – uh, I have this one too," squirmed Jonny, taking the comic and leafing through the pages. "Wait, this isn't right – it says he lives in a secret castle in the Antarctic. . ."

"Yeah, *Fortress Atomic*!" replied Vernon, excitedly. "That's where he does all his super-genius stuff and watches out for supervillainy and disasters and alien invaders and stuff."

"It says he has a robot butler. That's *stupid*," mumbled Jonny to himself as he flicked through the pages.

"Captain Atomic's super-clever, super-strong, super-*everything*," continued Vernon, obliviously. "He's probably the most powerful superhero ever. More powerful than Dyna-Max or Mr Megaton or Dr Probability. . ."

"Yeah, he's pretty cool, I guess," said Jonny, proudly.

"Did you hear he was battling Vinister Vile in Albion City this morning? Look, I get news updates on my phone," Vernon said, taking a mobile phone out of his pocket.

"Captain Atomic defeated his monster, but Vinister Vile got away. Did you know that he's the only villain that Captain Atomic's never managed to—"

DRiiiiiiiiiiiiiNG!

Jonny shuddered at the sound of the school bell. The thought of an afternoon with Ms Crackdown – and Tommy – filled him with dread.

"I wonder what the *other* teachers are like?" he sighed.

"I wonder if your brother will make it through the afternoon without getting us in any more trouble?" sighed Vernon.

"He'd *better*," growled Jonny.

THE STRANGE FATE OF SIR PERCIVAL

ALBION CHRONICLE

3RD SEPTEMBER

ATOMIC SAVES CAT IN TREE

Hero takes a break from saving world to save cat

"The real mystery is how they get up there," jokes superhero

As it happened, the rest of the day passed almost without incident. To Jonny and Ms Crackdown's surprise, Tommy suddenly seemed rather quiet – and rather ordinary. He was on his best behaviour. Ms Crackdown strode around the classroom, sniffing victoriously, confident that her strategy had worked – and she had crushed the will of yet another pupil.

"I do not like people," she scoffed as she wandered up and down. "But most of all, I do not like *children*. I cannot abide their ambition. 'I want to be an astronaut! I want to be a fireman! I want to be a princess! I want to be *extraordinary*.' Well, not on my watch, you don't."

Of course, Jonny knew his brother wasn't beaten. It was obvious Tommy was busy trying to work out Ms Crackdown's "weakness", but Jonny decided to ignore his sense of foreboding. He spent the afternoon working on an art project with Vernon, and even though Ms Crackdown had insisted that none of the projects would receive more than a D+, both boys had a fairly enjoyable afternoon.

"So what does your dad do?" asked Jonny as he added a few more explosions to their superhero picture.

"He works away," replied Vernon, a little sadly. "I don't get to see him very often."

"Something else we've got in common. I haven't seen my dad in *ages*," said Jonny. He held up the picture. "What do you reckon?"

"I dunno – needs something else," Vernon muttered. Jonny rolled up a piece of red paper and stuck it on the picture.

"If in doubt, add more explosions," he said.

"*Definitely*," giggled Vernon.

In the end, it was a satisfyingly ordinary afternoon all round.

That is, until *the scream*.

It was three minutes after the final school bell. All the children were pouring out of the school, and Jonny and Tommy were making their way through the car park to the village green.

"AAAAAH! My car! Where is it? Where is SIR PERCIVAL?"

Jonny spun around to see Ms Crackdown

in the school car park, yelling at the top of her voice and jumping up and down in an empty parking space.

"What's going. . ." murmured Jonny, and then the penny dropped. He turned to Tommy. "What did you do?"

"Who, me? Nothing! How could I have done? I didn't even leave my chair," replied Tommy with mock innocence. "Then again, I didn't have to. I just looked out of the window and saw it there in the car park. *Sir Percival. . .*"

"Who's – wait, you mean Ms Crackdown's car? Why would you—" began Jonny. Tommy winked and pointed upwards, towards the roof of the school. There, perched on the tip of the roof's peak, was a rusty, electric-blue car.

"Tommy . . . you *didn't*," whispered Jonny.

"I so did," said Tommy, at the exact moment that Emily Pebbles-Smyth from class 2B cried out, "Mummy! There's a car on the roof!", and everyone looked up.

"SIR PERCIVAL! NOOOO!" screamed Ms Crackdown.

A moment later, the shimmering air and the patch of flattened grass on the village green signified the Atomic Bomber's unseen arrival. The hatch opened and the boys hurried inside without being noticed.

"So, how was your first day?" asked Aunt Sandwich. Tommy looked back at Ms Crackdown running up and down the car park in dismay.

"Not too bad," he replied with a grin.

A HARD DAY AT WORK

3rd September

SUPER!

YOUR DAILY SUPERHERO GOSSIP COLUMN

Battle of the biceps!

ATOMIC and MIGHT-MAN arm wrestle for charity

Four minutes later, the boys and Aunt
Sandwich were back on Atomic
Island and gathered in
the Control Centre.
A perturbed Uncle
Dogday was
pacing up
and down.

"Let me get this straight. On your very first day at school, you put your teacher's car on top of the school roof?" said Uncle Dogday.

"It was an accident," said Tommy.

"Liar! How can you put a car on a roof by accident?" yelled Jonny, unable to contain himself. "You thought school was a stupid idea, so you decided to ruin everything and make sure we couldn't go back."

"That's not true!" replied Tommy. "Crackdown is horrible to everyone and it's not *fair*. Dad says if something's not fair then you should *do* something about it. You don't see him letting Vinister Vile get away with being villainous – or Techno Tyrant or Madface or Professor Repressor, or any of them!"

"But Ms Crackdown's not a supervillain!" growled Jonny.

"That's quite enough shouting from both of

you – we schnauzers have very sensitive hearing," interjected Uncle Dogday. "Now, while there is no excuse for this kind of behaviour, I can't pretend it's unexpected. I do realize how hard it is for both of you, trying to fit in after a lifetime of virtual solitude. What's more, it looks like your father is tied up with a tidal wave for the moment, so he won't be home for dinner. I suggest, therefore, that we draw a line underneath today's events, and start again afresh tomorrow."

"WHAT? THAT'S IT?

You're just going to let him get away with it?" cried Jonny.

"Not at all – Tommy will have double chores for the next month," replied Uncle Dogday.

"Double chores?" repeated a horrified Tommy. "But—"

"But nothing," snapped Uncle Dogday. "Your

father has defeated Vinister Vile, plugged an erupting volcano, foiled seventeen bank robberies, cured hiccups and saved a cat from a tree. I for one do not want to burden him with this on top of everything. Now, I think that's quite enough squabbling for one day. Go and wash your hands for dinner."

"We're having pizza!" added Aunt Sandwich, doing her best to lighten the mood.

"I'm not hungry," huffed Jonny. "Tommy can have it – he always gets what he wants anyway."

And with that, Jonny strode up the stairs and out of the Control Centre. When he reached his room, he closed the door and didn't come out until the following morning.

DAY TWO:

THROG,
THE HUNDRED-EYED HORROR

Albion Times, *4th September*

VINISTER STRIKES AGAIN!
**City attacked by second monster in two days
"Oh, for goodness' sake," remark
fleeing residents**

By the time Jonny woke up, his dad was already
battling another of Vinister Vile's mutated
monstrosities, Throg (the hundred-eyed horror),
in Albion City.

It wasn't the only crisis to befall a member of
the Atomic family.

"We've run out of milk," said Tommy, who was standing outside Jonny's bedroom door when he opened it. "Are you all right with toast? Or there's leftover pizza. I saved you some," he added.

"Toast's fine – thanks," grunted Jonny, adding, "You're up early. . ."

"Double chores, remember? I've been recalibrating the Island's imperceptors," said Tommy. "Oh yeah, and Dad's fighting another monster, so Aunt Sandwich is going to take us to school *again*. There's always something. . ."

The first thing the boys noticed when they arrived at school was that Ms Crackdown's car was no longer on the roof (although there was an enormous crane in the car park, which had presumably been used to "rescue" Sir Percival). Neither boy said anything. Jonny and Tommy just decided to pretend it had never happened and hope that everyone else had done the same.

They hadn't.

"How did it get up there?"

"Did anyone see it?"

"Buzz Bulldrop's mum said a tornado put it there!"

"Eddie Spink's cousin said it was a whirlwind!"

"Tornado!"

"Whirlwind!"

"Vortex!"

"Space alien!"

"Maybe it was a *supervillain*," said Vernon, catching up with Jonny and Tommy as they were walking to their classroom. Vernon still had his water pistol clipped to his belt and was waving a comic book around. "See, in issue 112 of Captain Atomic comics, Vinister Vile uses his ray gun, Vile's Violator, to teleport the Atomic-mobile to the top of a skyscraper!"

"Wait, the *Atomic-mobile?*" chuckled Tommy. "There's no such thing as—"

"Vernon is Captain Atomic's number one fan," said Jonny, nudging Tommy in the ribs. "He knows *everything* about him."

"Do you know they're fighting right now?" said Vernon, showing them a news report on his phone. "The Albion City news says Vinister Vile's new monster knocked Captain Atomic through a building – BLAM!"

"You shouldn't believe everything you read," said Tommy, defensively. He pushed past Vernon to get into the classroom. "Anyway, I don't see you saving the world with your water pistol. Maybe you should get your facts straight before pretending to know anything about my – about Captain Atomic."

"I didn't. . . Sorry," squeaked a nervous Vernon.

"Tommy! Leave him alone," said Jonny, sternly.

"Oh, so you and Four-eyes are best friends now? That was quick," huffed Tommy. "Fine. Have fun. I've got better things to do anyway."

A tense moment later, Ms Crackdown strode into the room and deathly silence fell about the class. She stood in front of her desk, looking more fearsome than ever.

"I assume by now that you termites all know what happened to my car," she hissed. "My trusty steed, my blue knight, my beloved Sir Percival."

Tommy's shoulders began to shudder as he giggled silently.

"I don't know how Sir Percival got there, but I know for a fact that it wasn't the weather. Someone, yes, some*one*, *put* him up there. Rest assured, I will uncover the culprit, and I will make them *pay*."

"Maybe it was a whirlwind," said Tommy.

Ms Crackdown glared at him. "Have you forgotten the ants' nest?" she hissed. "The actions of one affect the whole. So, until the culprit admits their crime, you will *all* be punished! All break times are *cancelled*. All lunches will be eaten silently in the classroom. All lessons will be maths. Maths, maths and more maths – until you have numbers, fractions and functions coming out of your ears. And for those of you who actually *like* maths – no maths! You shall write poetry! And, miracle of miracles, if any of you excel at both, I will sit you in a corner with your face to the wall until you promise never to do well again."

As the class shivered in fear, Jonny glanced over at his brother to see a broad smile spreading across his face. Tommy was now more convinced than ever that their dad had sent them here to deal with Ms Crackdown's "villainy". He was going to prove that he had what it took to be a hero.

He was going to defeat her, once and for all.

CRACKING DOWN

THE BABBLEBROOK BABBLE
4th September

SOMETHING ACTUALLY HAPPENS IN BABBLEBROOK

Car found on top of school may be first actual

"occurrence" in village history

"It all seems a bit much," says man with dog

Tommy put his plan to defeat "The Evil Ms Crackdown" (as he was now calling her) into effect straight away. He spent the morning moving objects around her desk with his mind. Pens, staplers, cups, reading glasses – whatever she put down, he would move. By the end of the morning, she had tried to mark an essay with a cup of tea and tried to drink out of a pen holder and poked herself in the nose with a ruler. She looked ready to pull out her bright red hair in frustration.

But that wasn't enough for Tommy. It all seemed so small-scale after the "incident" with the car. He longed for the chance to defeat his first proper enemy – and prove to his dad that he was ready to be a superhero.

It wasn't until 11.28 a.m. that Tommy spotted his opportunity. He had spent the last ten minutes rolling Ms Crackdown's favourite pen off her desk with his mind. Finally, in a fit of anger and confusion, Ms Crackdown had shoved the pen inside her desk drawer only for Tommy to focus his power and fling the drawer out of the desk, sending its contents clattering to the floor with a

CRASH!

"Eyes down!" shrieked a befuddled Ms Crackdown. "Get on with your work, fleas!"

Tommy surveyed the contents of the drawer as Ms Crackdown picked them up. One item caught his eye. It was bright red and looked like some sort of dead animal. It took him a moment to realize what he was looking at.

"No *way*," he whispered, grinning widely. "I've got her!"

Two minutes *before* Ms Crackdown's desk drawer had crashed to the floor, Jonny had been halfway through writing an essay entitled "Why I'm Not Special" when he felt a tap on the shoulder. He turned to see Vernon prodding him with his water pistol.

"Did you hear? Vinister Vile escaped again!" whispered Vernon, waving his phone. "Captain Atomic defeated his monster, but Vile got away."

"See? I told you Atomic would beat him,"

whispered Jonny. "He always does."

"But Vinister Vile is the baddest villain ever – worse than The Overlorder or Dr Nightmare Scenario or anyone!" replied Vernon. "He's never even been caught – not once!"

Jonny had never met anyone so excited about his dad's superheroics. Imagine how excited he'd be if he knew who "Jonny Smith" really was! Despite himself, Jonny began to wonder if he could ever share his secret. He was sure he could trust Vernon – after all, he was Atomic's number one fan. No one would have to know, not even—

CRASH!

Ms Crackdown's desk drawer had crashed to the floor! Jonny immediately glanced over at his brother.

"What are you up to?" hissed Jonny. Then he saw the smug look on Tommy's face and knew the day was going to get a lot worse.

"I'm about to step up Operation: Defeat the Evil Ms Crackdown." replied Tommy.

"Whatever you're planning – don't!" whispered Jonny, as Tommy focused his power.

"And here . . . we . . . go!"

"SILENCE, I said! I will not tolerate. . ." snarled Ms Crackdown, until she heard the entire class gasp in unison as her *hair* popped off her head and floated into the air.

It was a *wig*! Ms Crackdown was completely bald!

"What – what's happening?" squealed Ms Crackdown, slapping her hands over her hairless head. She watched in horror as her hair floated over the heads of the children. The pupils' astonished gasps soon turned to giggles, and their giggles quickly turned to laughter. Ms Crackdown stood frozen and helpless.

"Tommy!" whispered Jonny, as Tommy moved the wig across the room with his mind. When it was almost above his head, Tommy stood up.

Jonny growled "Sit down!" but for Tommy, it wasn't enough to defeat his enemy. He had to look her in the eyes, so she would know it was him – even if she couldn't prove it. He guided the wig over his head, and then plucked it out of the air.

"Ms Crackdown?" he grinned. "I think this belongs to you."

ANOTHER DAY, ANOTHER DEFEAT

CITY VIEW 4th September

CATCH ME IF YOU CAN

ATOMIC ARCH-FOE VINISTER VILE DISAPPEARS AGAIN

"I'll get him next time!" pledges Atomic
as he saves coachload of school children

News quickly spread through the school about the floating wig. Amusement turned to suspicion, especially after the business with the car on the roof. By the end of the day, the whole school was filled with talk of ghosts and hauntings.

"Did you see the look on her face?" said Tommy for the fifth time, as the Bomber docked on Atomic Island.

"Leave. Me. Alone," grunted Jonny.

"What's wrong with you?" shouted Tommy, as Jonny stormed off. "Crackdown's never going to show her face at school again! I've saved you a year of misery!"

"I do hate to see you two arguing," said Aunt Sandwich. "What did you actually *do*, Tommy?"

"I just did what Dad would have done. I won," replied Tommy.

"SHUT UP!" said Jonny, wheeling around. Jonny zoomed at super-speed back down the corridor and pinned Tommy against the wall. "You have no idea how Dad thinks!

He'd never want you to – to torture an old lady! Dad spends his whole life thinking of other people! You just think about yourself!"

"Oh me, oh my – can't we just agree to disagree?" squeaked Aunt Sandwich.

"So if Dad only thinks about other people, how come he never thinks about *us*?" spat Tommy. "I mean, there's always some idiot on TV, all smiling and happy because Dad saved them or opened their hospital or saved their stupid cat. Everybody else gets to see him more than we do!"

"Is that what this is about?" growled Jonny. "Are you being a total *idiot* just so Dad will pay you more attention?"

"No!" replied Tommy. "I'm just . . . *sick* of no one knowing who we are. Dad was famous by the time he was three years old! Why do we have to pretend to be ordinary when he gets to be special?"

"I keep telling you, I don't *want* to be special!" spat Jonny.

"Yeah? Well, you're an *Atomic* – you don't get to choose," said Tommy.

"Not when you're around, I don't!" yelled Jonny, and for the second time in two days, he stormed to his room, slammed the door and (despite the temptation of Aunt Sandwich's spaghetti bolognese and a game of fetch with Uncle Dogday) did not come out until the following morning.

DAY THREE:

REPUGNO, THE LIVING SWAMP THAT EATS EVERYTHING

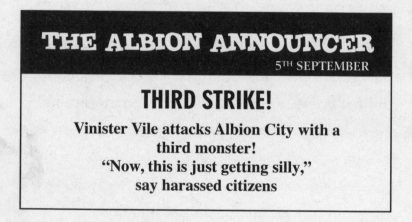

THE ALBION ANNOUNCER

5TH SEPTEMBER

THIRD STRIKE!

**Vinister Vile attacks Albion City with a
third monster!
"Now, this is just getting silly,"
say harassed citizens**

Jonny and Tommy didn't speak to each other until the Atomic Bomber had dropped them off at school and disappeared into the sky.

"You'll thank me, you know," said Tommy, finally, as he and Jonny strolled across the village green. "Now Crackdown's gone, you'll get your shot at that 'normal' life."

"Don't count on it," replied Jonny, pointing. In the doorway of the school stood Ms Crackdown, wig in place, and looking more fearsome than ever.

"Oh, come *on*. What's it going to take?" Tommy sighed in frustration. He took a defiant breath and strode towards her. "Morning, miss. You look different. Have you done something to your hair?"

"Come with me, Twin B. I have a unique assignment for you today," she said, grimly. "Something to keep you occupied and out of my hai – out of my *way* for quite some time."

Jonny shook his head. This wasn't going to end well. Still, he did like the idea of Tommy being out of trouble-causing proximity for a while. He watched Ms Crackdown lead his brother away and crossed his fingers that today would be the day that nothing bad happened.

"Jonny!" said Vernon, running up to him. "Did you hear? Atomic and Vinister Vile are fighting again! Vinister Vile's smashed up half of Albion City!"

Yeah, Dad was meant to be back for breakfast. Stupid Vinister Vile! thought Jonny. Then he saw the panic on Vernon's face and remembered that not everyone automatically expected his dad to win all his battles.

"Don't worry, Vernon, I'm sure Captain Atomic will be fine," he said. "He's handled Vinister Vile before, right?"

"Yeah, but what if it's not? What if – what if something. . ." began Vernon, fiddling with his water pistol.

"Look, everything's going to be OK. I *know* what I'm talking about."

"What do you mean?" asked Vernon. Jonny was

bursting to tell Vernon that he'd seen his father return from a hundred battles without so much as a scratch, but he couldn't. He thought again about sharing his secret. If anyone would understand who he really was, surely it was Vernon.

"Just . . . trust me," said Jonny finally, as they wandered into school. "And keep me posted, OK? Atomic's my favourite superhero too."

"Will do," said Vernon with a smile. "Hey, where's your brother?"

"Who knows?" replied Jonny. "Wherever Ms Crackdown's taken him, I just hope he stays out of trouble."

In fact, Ms Crackdown had led Tommy all the way to Babblebrook Primary's newly built fitness complex. She took him through the large gymnasium, full of equipment and lined with wooden benches. She then ushered him through a thick door labelled SWIMMING POOL.

"Cool," said Tommy. "Can I go swimming?"

"Of course not," replied Ms Crackdown. "You might enjoy yourself, and we can't have that. No, you are going to be brought into line. You are going to clean every toilet in this school. Starting here."

She pointed to the far end of the room. There were two more doors, marked BOYS and GIRLS.

"What? I'm not cleaning toilets!" protested Tommy as Ms Crackdown ushered him inside the boys' toilets.

"Oh, but you are," said Ms Crackdown. "I want every sink, floor, urinal and cubicle scrubbed until it gleams. You will work until the end of the day, or until the job is done."

"But . . . that's not fair!" said Tommy.

"And I told you, you little louse, I shall not tolerate defiance of any kind," Ms Crackdown replied. "But I am not without mercy. You will, of course, be given cleaning materials. Now where did I put them? Ah yes. . ."

Ms Crackdown reached into the pocket of her jacket and took out a small teacup . . . and a toothbrush.

"You've *got* to be kidding," groaned Tommy.

"You will clean the toilets with a toothbrush and a cup of water. And who knows? Perhaps with you in here, all these strange occurrences might stop," said Ms Crackdown. "I shall be back at lunch time – I expect your toothbrush to be worn to a nub by then."

Then with an uncharacteristic grin, Ms Crackdown turned on her heels and left.

Tommy stared at the toothbrush. He could probably use his powers to speed things along, but using superpowers to clean toilets still involved cleaning toilets. He had to think of a way to turn the situation to his advantage – a way to defeat her, once and for all. He made his way back into the gym, his mind racing. Then his eyes fixed upon door to the swimming pool. Like a bolt from the blue, he remembered something Ms Crackdown had said on their first day at Babblebrook Primary.

Something about a *crocodile*. . .

THE CURIOUS INCIDENT OF THE
CROCODILE IN THE SWIMMING POOL

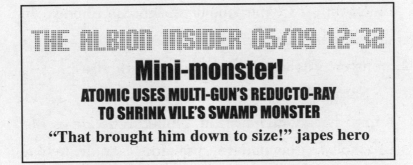

By lunch time, Jonny still hadn't seen any sign of Tommy. Despite enjoying a relatively "ordinary" morning, he was getting a little concerned about his brother. Instead of heading to lunch, he and Vernon carefully followed Ms Crackdown outside. They stayed a safe distance away as she made her way towards the fitness centre.

"You don't think Ms Crackdown got *rid* of him, do you?" whispered Vernon.

"What do you – no!" said Jonny. "Not that she could if she wanted to. . . ."

"Look!" said Vernon, checking his phone. "It says Atomic has defeated Vinister Vile's swamp monster! Vile's on the run! Do you think—"

"Shhh! She's going into the fitness centre," said Jonny. They watched from behind a hedge as Ms Crackdown reached for the door handle, when the door swung open . . . to reveal a distressed-looking Tommy on the other side. Jonny and Vernon watched in amazement as he flung his arms around Ms Crackdown.

"*Now* what's he up to?" whispered Jonny.

"Oh, Ms Crackdown, thank goodness!" cried Tommy, hugging Ms Crackdown in mock terror. "You've got to come quickly! There's . . .

something in the pool."

"What are you talking about?" said an impatient Ms Crackdown as Tommy dragged her into the gym.

"I was cleaning the toilets just like you said, and I heard a noise . . . coming from in here. I went to look and I saw something *weird*."

"You had better not be messing with me, Twin B – I don't like mess," said Ms Crackdown. She swung open the swimming pool door and strode into the dimly lit room.

"Stupid little slug. There's nothing here!" she barked.

"No. . . Look *in* the pool," said Tommy. Ms Crackdown peered into the pool. She could make out a very large, very dark shadow at the bottom. She stepped to the edge of the pool and leaned over to get a closer look. She wondered if it was a bench – that is, until it *moved*. The shape had started to swim to the far end of the pool.

"Oh no!" she cried. A second later, a massive crocodile propelled itself out of the water! It landed on the edge of the pool and dragged itself further on to the side.

"See? *Told* you there was something in the pool," chuckled Tommy.

"Cro – cro – croc—" whimpered Ms Crackdown, beside herself with terror. The beast swung its huge head, fixing its stare on Ms Crackdown.

"**CROCODILE!!**" screamed Ms Crackdown.

JONNY VS CROCODILE

THE CHIT-CHAT 05/09

A VILE CHILDHOOD
ARE VINISTER VILE'S WICKED WAYS DUE
TO A LACK OF GOOD PARENTING?

"If only his dad had hugged him,
the world wouldn't be in constant peril," say experts

Jonny may not have been an actual superhero, but he knew the difference between a regular scream and a "Save me!" scream. This was definitely the latter.

"Stay here, Vernon," he said. The boys had already snuck around the back of the fitness centre, looking for a way to see what Tommy was up to.

"But where are you going?" replied Vernon.

"Just stay here!" yelled Jonny. He was already running around the other side of the fitness centre. Once he was sure Vernon could no longer see him, he leapt, in a single bound, up on to the roof! He scrambled up to the skylight and peered down, to see Ms Crackdown running at full pelt.

"AAAAAAAHHH!" she screamed.

"What's she running from?" muttered Jonny. A moment later, he got his answer – a massive crocodile burst through the doorway to the swimming pool! It was already moving much faster than Ms Crackdown – she'd never make it out of the gym in time!

Jonny grabbed the skylight and tore it off the roof, then leapt through the hole into the gym. He landed right in front of the crocodile just as it got within chomping distance of Ms Crackdown.

The beast immediately opened its jaws to bite but Jonny grabbed hold, a jaw in each hand.

The crocodile thrashed and shook its head with all its might, but Jonny held on. He turned to see Ms Crackdown racing towards the school, and hoped she did not look back to see him wrestling with the giant reptile.

That DOES it. . .

Vernon was lying on the floor, covered in huge chunks of debris, with a trickle of blood rolling down his forehead.

"Oh no. . ." whispered Jonny, dropping the sink. He rushed over to Vernon and carefully cleared the chunks of shattered wall.

"He must have climbed in through the window . . . I told him to wait. . ." said Jonny, distraught. "Vernon, are you OK? I'm sorry! Talk to me!"

"He's hurt, Jonny," said Tommy. "We have to get him to the Island. *Now*."

"We – we can't," whimpered Jonny. "The secret!"

"Forget the secret," said Tommy. "Look at him. This is our fault. We have to fix this, right—"

"Tommy! Are you there?" cried a familiar voice. "Hold on, I'm coming! I'll save you!"

"Ms Crackdown?" said Tommy. He poked his

head out of the hole in the changing room wall. There was Ms Crackdown at the gymnasium door, desperately trying to open the locked door.

"What's she doing? Why did she come back?" muttered Tommy.

"I could be wrong," began Jonny, "but I think she's trying to *save* you."

"Why?" asked Tommy.

"Maybe she's not as evil as you think," said Jonny, activating his Atomic Clock. "There! Aunt Sandwich will be here in a few minutes. Let's go!"

"*You* go. Get Vernon back to Atomic Island," said Tommy. "I'll stay here and handle Crackdown."

"No – no way! No more you versus Ms Crackdown!" said Jonny.

"Look, we can't let her back in here with an angry crocodile, can we?" replied Tommy. "I'll be good – I'll do what I'm told. No tricks. This time, I'll take whatever's coming to me."

"Really? But how are you going to explain all this?" asked Jonny, looking around at the wreckage.

"Let me worry about that," replied Tommy. "Go!"

Jonny scooped Vernon into his arms.

"Good luck, Tommy."

Jonny kicked a hole in the changing room wall and sped out. Tommy clambered back into the gym just as Ms Crackdown started banging on the front door with her stick. Tommy composed himself and then strolled to the door and opened it.

"You're alive! Oh, thank goodness! Run, Tommy, quickly! I'll protect you!" she cried, her face white with panic. After a moment, she noticed the devastated gymnasium. "Wait –

where is the crocodile? What *happened* here?"

"Actually, it's sort of a long story. . ." replied Tommy.

SECRETS' OUT

ZOO-NEWS.COM

ONE OF OUR CROCODILES IS MISSING

Giant man-eating croc disappears from enclosure
"We advise everyone to panic," say zoo staff

"Owww..." moaned Vernon as he woke up. He felt a dull pain over his eye. He reached up to his head to find it wrapped in bandages. He slowly opened his eyes – and saw a dog and a hamster staring back at him.

"What's happening?" he muttered, looking around. He was in a long white room full of beds. It was like a hospital ward, but without the funny smell.

"You took quite a bump to the head, young man," said the dog.

"AAAH!" screamed Vernon. "Talking dog!"

"Dogday, don't upset the boy," said Aunt Sandwich.

"**AAAH!**" screamed Vernon again. "Talking gerbil!"

"*Gerbil?*" cried Aunt Sandwich, indignantly. "Oh me, oh my, no! How many gerbils do you know that can talk?"

"I'm *really* not looking forward to explaining this to the Captain. . ." sighed Uncle Dogday.

"It's OK, Vernon, everything's fine," said a voice. Vernon looked around to see Jonny smiling back at him.

"What's going on?" blurted Vernon. "I heard noises in the gym. I climbed through a window, and then. . ."

"Then we smashed through the wall and landed on you. Sorry about that," said Jonny.

"Smashed through the wall? What do you – wait, where *am* I?" asked a nervous Vernon.

"It's probably easier if I show you," said Jonny. He helped Vernon off the bed and carefully guided him to a nearby window. Vernon looked out to see a huge expanse of sky, and an orange sun setting in the distance. He looked down at the city below.

"That's – that's Albion City," he said, agog. "I recognize it from the comics. . ."

"They get *some* things right," said Jonny. "The thing is, my name isn't Jonny Smith. It's Jonny *Atomic*."

"Atomic? Your name is. . . You mean, like Captain Atomic?"

"I just call him Dad," replied Jonny with a shrug.

"No WAY," said Vernon.

One long explanation later and Vernon was up to speed on Jonny and Tommy's secret. It seemed like the least Jonny could do after almost killing him, and it felt surprisingly good, being able to tell him the truth.

"And check *this* out," said Jonny, proudly, as they made their way into a huge chamber bathed in red light and filled with machinery. In the centre, a huge cylinder stood ten metres tall, glowing and sparking with bright crimson energy. Jonny grinned as Vernon stared at it in awe. "This is what keeps Atomic Island in the air."

"Do you really have to give the guided tour?" winced Uncle Dogday. "It's bad enough he's here at all."

"Don't worry, we can trust him. Vernon's my *friend*," said Jonny, proudly. "Plus, he's Dad's biggest fan! He's got, like, a *million* Atomic comics. He's even got a water pistol like Dad's multi-gun. Go on, Vernon, show them!"

Vernon took his water pistol off his belt and held it up.

"What fun!" chuckled Aunt Sandwich.

Vernon pointed at the cylinder of energy. "How does it work?"

"The Core is a clean, perpetual energy source," said Uncle Dogday. "It has been powering the Island for more than forty years, keeping it invisible and keeping it aloft."

"But if something *happened* to it – I mean, if it was damaged?"

"Oh me, oh my, don't panic!" said Aunt Sandwich.

"Quite so, Aunt Sandwich," replied Uncle Dogday, pointing out of a high window into the clear blue sky. "After all, no one out there even knows the Island exists. . ."

"Vernon, are you OK?" asked Jonny. "You look funny. Is it your head?"

"I'm fine," replied Vernon. He pointed the water pistol at Jonny. "I'm just . . . *sorry*."

"Sorry?" repeated a baffled Jonny. "What for?"

THE VENGEANCE OF VERNON VILE

VILE'S LAST STAND?

Villain cornered in power
station by Atomic

"Vernon . . . *Vile?*" wheezed a paralysed Jonny. "You mean . . . your dad is Vinister Vile?"

"Yup," nodded Vernon.

"Oh me, oh my!" cried Aunt Sandwich, helpless in Vernon's grip.

"Are you going to keep saying that? It's *really* annoying," said Vernon.

"But you *love* Captain Atomic!" said Jonny.

"You know all about him you have his comics – you have his multi-gun!"

"Actually, this is a Vile's Violator, my dad's weapon of choice," said Vernon, waving his "water pistol" around. "I guess you must have thought I was pretty obsessed with your dad – but I would be, wouldn't I? My dad's spent *years* fighting your dad, trying to find ways to beat him. Defeating the mighty Captain Atomic is all he thinks about. He's spent more time doing that than he has with me. He doesn't care what I do. Do you know I built this gun myself? I'm not even ten years old, and *I built my own ray gun*! But do you think my dad even notices?"

"I'm sure he's just been busy . . . trying to kill my dad and stuff," said Jonny.

"In the end I think I just got in the way of his plans, so he packed me off to school," sighed Vernon. "Sometimes I feel like he doesn't even know I exist. . ."

"Vernon, I know how you feel, I do. . ." began Jonny, but Vernon wasn't listening.

"But now – now I finally have a way to impress him. If I *destroy* Atomic Island, there's no way he can ignore me."

"No! Vernon, you can't!" cried Jonny, as he felt his fingers twitch.

"Sorry, Jonny," said Vernon. "If he finds out I had the chance to do this and I didn't, he's going to ground me for *ages*."

Vernon adjusted the power settings on his gun and pointed it at the Core.

"Vernon, DON'T!" cried Jonny and Aunt Sandwich together, but it was too late – Vernon fired.

zAKOW!

The whole room juddered as the Core began to pulse and dim. Red bolts forked across the room like lightning. The whole Island shook and groaned as its gravitators and imperceptors drained of power. The floor began to tilt – until the city below them was clearly visible in the window.

"You're a very bad boy!" snapped Aunt Sandwich.

"It's nothing personal, honest," replied Vernon. "Jonny, you've got twenty minutes before the Core completely loses power and the Island falls. You'll probably have enough feeling back in your legs to make a run for it before the Island crashes!"

"No, stop! Put me down! JONNY!" cried Aunt Sandwich as Vernon raced towards the hangar bay.

"Vernon! STOP!" yelled a still-frozen Jonny, sliding across the floor as the Island tipped on its axis.

Twenty minutes. . . he thought. *Twenty minutes before the Island crashes into the city, killing hundreds of people.*

Jonny cast his eyes down to his hand. His fingers were twitching. If he could only move them enough to reach his Atomic Clock, he could contact his brother.

But of course, Tommy had problems of his own.

DETENTION TENSION

THE BABBLEBROOK BABBLE
5th *September*

LET'S JUST CARRY ON AS NORMAL

Residents choose to ignore weird goings-on at local school

"I'd rather just pretend it didn't happen,"

says woman with moustache

One hundred and ninety-nine kilometres east of the plummeting Atomic Island, Babblebrook Primary School had been evacuated "due to crocodile". The police had arrived to cordon off the area and the zoo had been summoned to collect its missing reptile. The children, staff and onlookers gathered outside the school for the second time that week.

Only two people remained inside the school. Ms Crackdown had refused to leave until she got to the bottom of this mystery, so Tommy wasn't going anywhere.

"So you're trying to tell me that a crocodile destroyed the gymnasium?" said Ms Crackdown, pacing up and down her classroom. "And then it managed to get itself wrapped up in a curtain, after which it locked itself in the swimming pool room?"

"Yes, Ms Crackdown," said Tommy, meekly.

"Lies upon lies!" hissed Ms Crackdown. "You bring chaos wherever you go, you little cockroach. And now this – destruction of school property. You have crossed a line and we will have to make an example of you. You'll be cleaning toilets with toothbrushes for a year!"

Tommy knew Ms Crackdown was right. There was only so much he could blame on an escaped crocodile. It had gone too far. This time, he would just have to take whatever was coming to him. He sighed, bowed his head. . .

A red light was blinking on his Atomic Clock.

"The emergency signal!" whispered Tommy. He remembered what Aunt Sandwich had told them about only using the watches in dire emergencies – and he knew that Jonny always did *exactly* as he was told. Something was very wrong.

"Um, Ms Crackdown?"

"Woodlouse! Raise your hand if you wish to speak!" shrieked Ms Crackdown. Tommy shook his head and raised his hand.

"Yes?" hissed Ms Crackdown.

"Um. . . Please, Ms Crackdown, I really have to go," began Tommy. "It might be sort of important."

"Is that the best you can do?" scoffed Ms Crackdown. "You expect me to let you spread your beetle wings and fly away?"

"I think my brother might be in trouble," said Tommy. "I promise – I properly promise I'll clean as many toilets as you want tomorrow, but right now, you *have* to let me go."

"You're wasting your breath," said Ms Crackdown with a crooked smile. "There is nothing you can say that will make me set you free."

Tommy sighed and stared again at his blinking Atomic Clock. He gritted his teeth, not quite able to believe what he was going to do. But what other choice did he have? He looked out of the window, at the gathered crowds, the police, the cars in the car park. He held his breath and concentrated.

"You know, sometimes, people really are extraordinary," said Tommy. "Look out of the window."

"The more you tell yourself that, the more difficult your life will be," said Ms Crackdown, peering out of the window. Suddenly, every car in the car park began to shake and judder. A moment later, the cars began to float into the air! The onlookers began screaming and running for cover as thirty or more cars flew into the air and hovered there like they were weightless.

"My name is Tommy Atomic and I'm the son of Captain Atomic, the world's greatest superhero. Don't make me prove it by dropping Sir Percival."

"Impossible . . . remarkable . . . extraordinary!" whispered Ms Crackdown.

"Told you," smiled Tommy.

THE SAD TALE OF
MS CRACKDOWN

THE ALBION ADVISOR 05/09

Excuse me, is that your crocodile?

**Village school has unwelcome visitor in the shape
of five-metre reptile**

"That's it, time to move," say locals

"I'm the son of a superhero," said Tommy, proudly. "And I really have to go. . ."

"How could I have been so blind? Sir Percival . . . my hair . . . the crocodile. . .!" cried Ms Crackdown with an uncharacteristic laugh. "It was so obvious! Can it be? Has it been *so* long since I've been around superheroes that I've forgotten how to read the signs?"

"'Been around superheroes'? You mean, you *know* actual superheroes?" said Tommy.

"More than that," said Ms Crackdown, turning to face Tommy. She took a deep breath and raised her right hand. After a few seconds, Tommy saw her fingers crackle with electricity. She pointed and a tiny blue lightning bolt shot across the room and knocked over a chair!

Tommy was so shocked he dropped the cars in the car park! They landed with an almighty CRAASH! as he stared at the energy sparking and wheeling around Ms Crackdown's hand.

"It's been thirty-five years since I've done that. I wasn't sure I still had it in me," she said, smiling slightly.

"But what – how – huh?" babbled Tommy. "You have *superpowers*!"

"Forty years ago, I was known as The Blue Dynamo," continued Ms Crackdown. "I donned a cape and mask and fought alongside the superheroes of the time, fighting for truth, justice – all that nonsense. I was quite the celebrity back then. I thought I was the greatest superhero that ever lived. I didn't even mind that my electrical powers made my hair fall out. . ."

"I don't understand – you have superpowers! What are doing here? Why are you a teacher?" asked Tommy. Ms Crackdown sighed and sat down at her desk.

"It was at the height of my superhero career," she began. "The public adored me. I had even started to believe I was *better* than the people I fought to protect. Then, one day, I made a public appearance at a zoo. People came from miles around, all of them desperate to meet The Blue Dynamo."

"What happened?" asked Tommy, as curious as he was impatient to leave.

"I was so busy signing autographs, I didn't notice that a crocodile had escaped from its enclosure. It started breaking into other pens, causing havoc. People were screaming 'Help! Help!' but I just kept signing autographs.

All I cared about was being **EXTRAORDINARY**. By the time I finally realized what had happened, the crocodile had eaten two monkeys and a parakeet. I never forgave myself. I also developed a phobia of crocodiles, which wasn't actually a problem until today."

"That is officially the weirdest story I've ever heard," said Tommy, shaking his head.

"That was the day I gave up being a superhero. I swore never to use my powers again. Instead, I dedicated my life to making sure no one ever felt special or remarkable or extraordinary, so that no one would ever make the same mistakes I made. I became a teacher – and spent the next thirty years trying to keep people in their place."

"Uh, Ms Crackdown?" said Tommy, raising his hand again. "I *really* think my brother's in trouble. Could I go now? Um. . . Please?"

Ms Crackdown took another deep breath.

"Perhaps I have been too harsh. I see those monkeys and that poor parakeet every time I close my eyes and I try to honour their memories . . . but by golly, I'm not about to have another death on my conscience! Very well – go! Help your brother! But remember . . . our secrets must remain secrets. Tomorrow, I will be as bafflingly unpleasant to you as ever – and I expect you to do the same for me."

WELCOME HOME, CAPTAIN ATOMIC

The Unlikely Albion
GIANT METEOR TURNS BACK

Albion City not even slightly crushed by
enormous falling rock

Citizens "very pleased" not to be squished

"We're not out of trouble yet," said Jonny as he
helped an exhausted Tommy to his feet. "Vernon
kidnapped Aunt Sandwich! We've got to rescue
her, before—"

"Oh me, oh my, it's so nice to know you care!"
said a voice. The boys spun around to see Vernon
Vile with his hands in the air, reluctantly shuffling

back into the Core Chamber. And scurrying behind him, wielding his Vile's Violator in her tiny paws. . .

"Aunt Sandwich! You're OK!" cried Jonny. "But how did – how could – HOW?"

"You're not the only ones with tricks up your sleeves!" chuckled Aunt Sandwich. "You don't spend your whole life around superheroes without learning a thing or two about defeating supervillains."

"*Please* let me go!" cried Vernon. "I can't get caught on my first attempt at supervillainy. Dad'll kill me! He's been doing it for years and he's *never* been caught!"

"If your father is who I think he is, then that is no longer the case," said a deep, booming voice. Jonny and Tommy looked up at the smashed window to see Captain Atomic hovering in the air and carrying a handcuffed Vinister Vile under one mighty arm.

"DAD!" cried Jonny, Tommy and Vernon together, as Captain Atomic landed in the Core Chamber.

"Good to see you again, boys!" said the Captain. He dropped Vinister Vile on his bottom and hugged Jonny and Tommy tightly.

"Vernon? Is this some dreaded delusion? What in the name of doom and devastation are you doing at this destination?" asked a dazed Vinister.

"The same thing you are, by the looks of it, Dad," replied Vernon, shaking his head. "Getting *caught*."

"Sorry I didn't get to take you to school, boys," said Captain Atomic. "It's been a tough few days, what with one thing or another. So, what have I missed?"

Jonny and Tommy looked at each other and smiled.

"Nothing much," they said, shrugging.

In fact, the whole truth never *quite* came out about Jonny and Tommy's misadventures. Vernon was more than happy to take the blame for almost destroying the Island, as it impressed his dad so much! And, to Tommy's delight, Vernon also volunteered to take the blame for pretty much everything that had happened at Babblebrook Primary. The worse it was, the happier Vinister Vile became. Finally, Vernon's dad seemed genuinely proud of him. Just before Captain Atomic returned them to the surface (and into the hands of the authorities) Vernon looked at Jonny, who was tending to a dazed Uncle Dogday, and mouthed, "Thanks."

Jonny wasn't sure what to think, especially as he was still feeling the after-effects of Vernon's enfeebler beam, but he found himself raising his arm and giving Vernon the thumbs up.

With the Viles safely in custody, the Atomic family set to work repairing the Island and getting everything back to normal – or as normal as ever.

"Vernon Vile sounds like quite the master criminal," said Captain Atomic, surveying the

Core Chamber. "Causing havoc at school, finding his way on to the Island, defeating you all and nearly destroying the city! Supervillains are getting younger and younger these days."

"So are super*heroes*," said Uncle Dogday, nodding towards the boys, who were sweeping up pieces of the smashed window. Captain Atomic scratched his head and looked a bit awkward.

"Boys, I know I'm not around as much as I should be, and with your mother being in prison for supervillainy . . . things are difficult. But I want you to know I'm proud of you – you saved hundreds of lives today. I guess I've always tried to protect you from the *super* side of things, and to give you the chance to be ordinary for as long as you could. I don't know, maybe that was a mistake. Maybe. . ."

"Maybe we can be both," said Jonny.

"Listen to you!" scoffed Tommy. "You save one

little city and all of a sudden you think you're a *superhero*."

"Tell you what," said their dad. "You keep going to school, and we'll talk – just talk – about starting your *real* training."

"Sounds good to me," said Tommy.

"What? I thought you hated school," Jonny said.

"It's starting to grow on me," replied Tommy with a grin.

"By the way, I intercepted a news report about some strange sightings over Babblebrook village today," added Captain Atomic. "Something about a *low-flying crocodile*. Either of you know anything about that?"

Tommy and Jonny smiled at each other, and then shook their heads.

"Didn't think so," said the boys' dad, with a wry smile.

DAY FOUR:
PLAGUE OF THE PLUNDERER

Albion City Telegraph

6TH SEPTEMBER (EARLY EDITION)

EVERYTHING BACK TO NORMAL (HOPEFULLY)

Albion City residents "really quite tired" of monster attacks

It was the same day that THE-INCREDIBLY-AWESOME-AND-ALMIGHTY-TOTAL-AND-DEFINITE-PLANETARY-CONQUEROR-EMPEROR-KING-OF-EVERYTHING began his conquest of earth. Fortunately, his only power was to think up impressive supervillain names, so he never actually left his living room.

It was also the day that Ms Crackdown decided that she might go a *tiny* bit easier on her pupils at Babblebrook Primary School.

And it was the day that Captain Atomic finally took his children to school.

Well, almost.

"Eat up, boys!" said Captain Atomic, as the boys tucked into their morning cereal. "Five minutes till we leave for school."

"I can't believe he's actually taking us," whispered Tommy.

"Don't jinx it," replied Jonny.

BARK! BARK!

"Sorry to interrupt, Captain," said Uncle Dogday. "But we have a situation."

"What is it?" said Captain Atomic. A massive view screen appeared, showing footage of a bank under attack. It was being beset by what looked like a cross between a tank and a vacuum cleaner. The massive machine was *sucking* money and gold out of the bank by the *truckload*.

"It appears The Plunderer is up to his old tricks again – namely, stealing whatever he can get his hands on," said Uncle Dogday.

"Not for long," said Captain Atomic. He adjusted the settings on his multi-gun – and then caught sight of the expectant faces of Jonny and Tommy. "I'm sorry, boys, but—"

"No problem, Dad," said Jonny. "Go. Save the day!"

"Yeah, it's your turn, anyway," added Tommy. "We *totally* saved the day yesterday."

"I'll make it up to you," said the boys' dad. "Just as soon as The Plunderer is behind bars."

Jonny and Tommy swelled with pride as they watched Captain Atomic set off on another bold adventure. They smiled to each other as they straightened their ties and picked up their school bags. *Their* next adventure would have to wait. . .

At least until they got to school.

LOOK OUT FOR MORE

ATOM!C

ADVENTURES

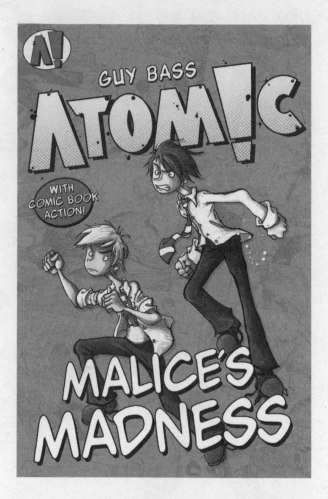